10
Cool Things
About Being a
Ring Bearer

Penelope Colville Paine

Itoko Maeno

In loving memory
John H. Paine 1935–2006

Published by
Paper Posie, Santa Barbara, CA
(800) 360–1761
See all Paper Posie's products for children at weddings at
www.paperposie.com

Publisher's Cataloging-in-Publication
(Provided by Quality Books, Inc.)

Paine, Penelope Colville, 1946-
   10 cool things about being a ring bearer / by Penelope C. Paine.
   — 1st ed.
   p.   cm.
ISBN-10: 0-9707944-2-8   ISBN-13: 978-0-9707944-2-0
   1. Wedding attendants—Juvenile literature. 2. Wedding etiquette—Juvenile
literature. [1. Weddings. 2. Weddings etiquette. 3. Etiquette.] I. Title.
II. Title: Ten cool things about being a ring bearer
BJ2065.W43P35 2002   395'.22
                                                            QBI33-391

Editor: Gail M. Kearns
Layout & Typography: Cirrus Book Design

Printed in China, Shenzhen, Guangdong
07/2015, C&C Offset Printing Co., Ltd.

18 19 20 21

This Book Belongs To:

_____

The Bride and Groom Will Be:

_____

Wedding Date:

_____

There are lots of cool things about
being a Ring Bearer . . .

1

A Ring Bearer is the groom's special helper

I was a ring bearer for my big brother. His wedding day was a Saturday. This is when I usually play soccer but I had lots of fun at the wedding.

2

A Ring Bearer gets to wear a really cool suit

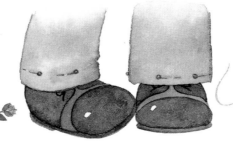

I wiggled a lot when I was being fitted for my ring bearer suit. My uncle had to help me stay still so that the tailor could fix the pants. I felt all grown up. On the wedding day I wore a bouttonnier.

3

A Ring Bearer carries the wedding
rings for the groom

I carried the rings on a ring pillow and I had to be very careful they didn't fall off.

4

The Ring Bearer gets to walk in front of the bride before the wedding ceremony and behind the bride and groom after they are married.

I knew I would have to walk very slowly so I wouldn't trip. At the rehearsal I had to practice going up and down the steps with the groomsmen. They said funny things and made me laugh.

5

A Ring Bearer is in the wedding ceremony

While the bride and groom were saying their vows, I stood as still as I could. Mom and Dad smiled at me and I felt very special. My dad squeezed my mom's hand when the groom kissed the bride.

6

A Ring Bearer makes new friends

I had to stand with my cousin. She was the Flower Girl. She carried a basket of rose petals. We had fun at the reception eating and dancing, and I stayed up very, very late.

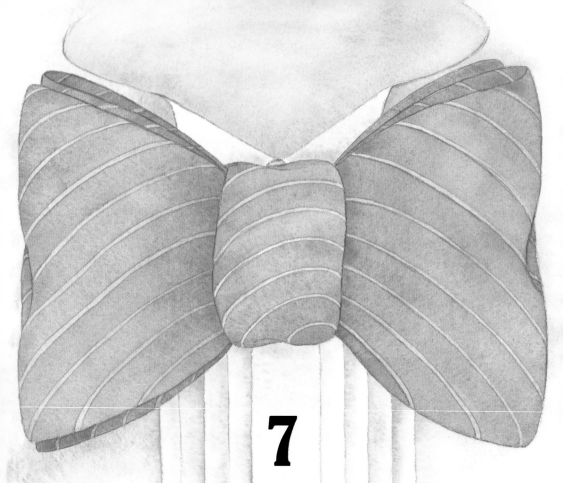

7

A Ring Bearer is in the wedding photographs

After the wedding ceremony we all threw rose petals over the bride and groom. I was in LOTS of photographs. Then we all went in a big limousine to the reception, where there was lots of yummy food and a band played!

8

A Ring Bearer gets a gift from the groom

JST MARRIED

Before the bride and groom went away on their honeymoon, the groom gave me a wrist-watch that I can even wear when I swim. I keep it in a box on the shelf in my bedroom.

Thanks Buddy!

9

A Ring Bearer gets to take home favors and treats

I took home balloons, bubbles, candy and even the frosting decoration from the wedding cake.

To
the Ring Bearer

10

A Ring Bearer has lots of fun with
his family and friends

I collected autographs
from all my relatives.
My aunt who lives far away
in another country gave me
$5.00 because I am saving up
to go to zoo camp in the
summer.

ZOO
CAMP

I liked being a Ring Bearer . . .
and I hope you do too!